A Little Wonder Reading Book

Hats
and
Cats

a division of
PRICE STERN SLOAN
Los Angeles

Hats and Cats

Written by
Roger Burrows
Illustrated by
Carole Etow
Edited by
Yvette Lodge

There once was a boy
who asked for a hat.
But what did they send him?
They sent him a cat!

There once was a boy
who asked for a hat,
then asked for a goat.
But what did they send him?
They sent him a boat!

There once was a boy
who lived on a boat.
He had a cat,
then asked for a house.
But what did they send him?
They sent him a mouse!

There once was a boy
who lived on a boat.
He had a cat
that chased a mouse.
To keep the mouse,
he asked for a box.
But what did they send him?
They sent him a fox!

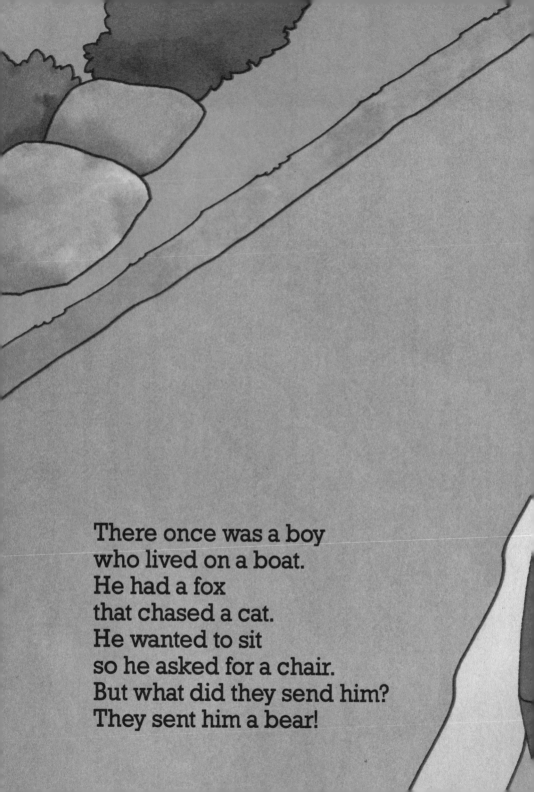

There once was a boy
who lived on a boat.
He had a fox
that chased a cat.
He wanted to sit
so he asked for a chair.
But what did they send him?
They sent him a bear!

There once was a boy
who lived on a boat
that sailed on a lake.
He had a bear
that chased a fox,
and he thought it would be funny
to ask for a bunny.
But what did they send him?
They sent him some honey!

There once was a boy
who lived on a boat
that sailed on a river.
He had a bear
that loved to eat honey,
and a fox that chased a cat.
He asked for an ox,
to chase the fox.
But what did they send him?
They sent him a box!

There once was a boy
who lived on a boat
that sailed out to sea.
He had a bear
that loved to eat honey,
and a fox that lived in a box.
He had a cat
that chased a mouse.
Then one day he asked for a dish.
But what did they send him?
They sent him some fish!

There once was a boy
who lived on a boat
that sailed on the sea.
He had a bear
that loved to eat honey,
and a fox that lived in a box.
He had a cat
that tried to catch fish,
and a mouse instead of a house.
Then he asked for a gentle breeze.
But what did they send him?
They sent him some cheese!

There once was a boy
who lived on a boat
that sailed on the sea.
He had a bear
that loved to eat honey,
and a fox that lived in a box.
He had a cat
that tried to catch fish,
and a mouse that liked to eat cheese.
Then he asked for a special wish—
to live happily ever after.
And what did his new friends do?
They made his wish come true!

LITTLE WONDER READING BOOKS

Enjoy all the delightful books in this series:

DINOSAUR DAYS

The Dinosaur Who Forgot Her Birthday

The Smallest Dinosaur In The World

The Dinosaur Who Wouldn't Go To School

The Dinosaur Who Couldn't Sleep

The Dinosaur Who Invented Things

The Dinosaur Who Wanted To Fly

RHYME, READ AND LEARN

The Land Of Colors

Hats And Cats

The Bouncing Ball

The Magic Clock

The Little White Cloud

Very Tall And Very Small